KHARI THE QUINOA
SAVES THE DAY

Jasmine Collier

PURPLE
VEGAN
MOMMa™

For my ever supportive family and for my purple people.

For information contact:
info@purpleveganmomma.com
Written by Jasmine Collier
Illustrated by Jasmine Collier and Ashini I. Samarathunga
ISBN: 978-1-957821-00-9
Library of Congress Control Number - 2022903665
Printed in the United States of America

It was a beautiful day at
Purple Vegan Momma's Market.

MUSHROOMS

LION'S MANE

LION'S MANE

TURKEY TAIL

TURKEY TAIL

REISHI

REISHI

FARM FRESH

ORANGES

ORGANIC

STRAWBERRIES

ORGANIC

NON GMO

NON GMO

Purple people were
busy shopping for
healthy foods
to bring home
to their families.

Suddenly he heard a crash. "It sounds like someone needs help right now! Purple Vegan Momma's Market is super busy today! I'd better check it out!" he said.

Khari peeked out from his quinoa home.

Charlie Chick Peas had fallen off his shelf.
"Ouch! That hurt," he said.

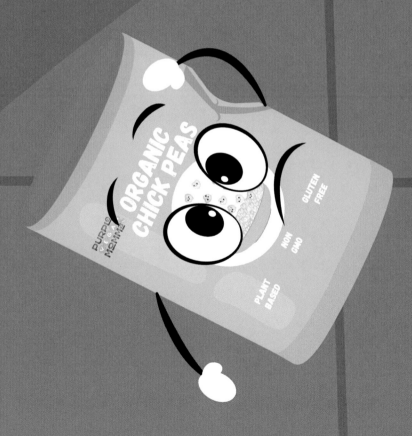

Khari darted through the air to help.

"I'm all bent," said Charlie Chick Peas sadly. Khari smiled and said "We all need to protect our soft delicate insides and your can did just that. You even have the dent to prove it!"

Khari whisked Charlie Chick Peas back
up to his shelf.

Charlie Chick Peas was given a warm welcome by all of his family and friends.

Suddenly Khari heard a fruit fall
from the produce section.

He raced over to the fallen fruit.

ORGANIC-NON GMO
PEARS

ORGANIC-NON GMO
WATERMELON

OR

♥ I LOVE YOU MY PURPLE F

Alan the Apple was sad.
"Look at my bruise!
No one will want me now,"
said Alan.

"All I see is how brightly you shine," said Khari.

Khari raced over to the freezer section.

Khari arrived and wondered, "Now who fell down?" He turned and saw the missing box of veggie burgers. "On my way!" he said as he pulled open the golden freezer doors.

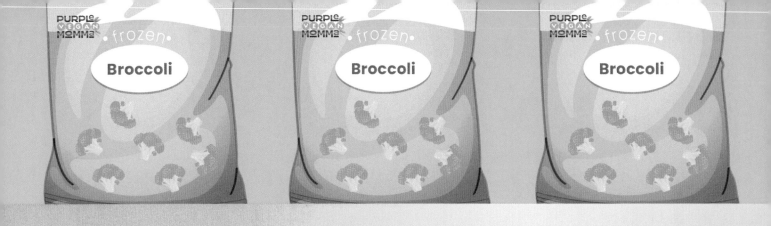

There at the bottom was Viktoria Veggie Burgers. "Khari, I'm so happy to see you! I laughed too hard and bounced right off my shelf. Now look at me! My box is ruined!" she cried. "Your box may be damaged but you're still cool as ice," said Khari.

They jetted through the freezing air. "Those icicles are no match for your warm heart," she said. Khari delivered Viktoria back home safely.

Outside the freezer,
Khari noticed that Purple Vegan
Momma's Market was dark.
"Look at that beautiful moon!
Time to get back home,"
he said.

Khari dashed through the aisles and climbed up to his quinoa home.

Khari was happy to be home again. He sat in his favorite chair, took a deep breath, and relaxed his mind.

Khari's heart glowed brightly as his own loving energy began to surround him. Calmly he said, "Purple Vegan Momma will be so proud. I can't wait to see what tomorrow brings."

Made in the USA
Middletown, DE
19 March 2025

72884231R00019